John Burningham

# CANNONBALL
# SIMP

RED FOX

for Lulu

A Red Fox Book

Published by Random House Children's Books
61–63 Uxbridge Road, London W5 5SA

A RANDOM HOUSE GROUP COMPANY
Addresses for companies within The Random House Group Limited
can be found at : www.randomhouse.co.uk/offices.htm

4 5 6 7 8 9 10

First published in Great Britain
by Jonathan Cape Ltd 1966
Red Fox edition 1999

Printed in Singapore

RANDOM HOUSE UK Limited Reg. No. 954009

ISBN 978-0-09-940077-6

Simp was what most people would call an ugly little dog.
She was fat and small, and had only a stump for a tail.
Her owner had found homes for her brothers and sisters
but could not persuade anybody to take Simp.
So, in order to get rid of her, he decided to leave her
somewhere, hoping that somebody would find her and
take her in.

One evening he took Simp outside the town and just dumped her near a rubbish pit.

Poor little Simp watched the van disappearing into the
distance. She did not know what to do. Then darkness
fell. By the light of the moon she explored the dump
and found an old armchair to spend the night in. Rats
came out and looked curiously at her. When Simp said
how hungry she was, one of them gave her a piece of
bread. "But you'll have to go in the morning," he said.
"It's hard enough for us rats to live. There wouldn't be
enough food for you as well."

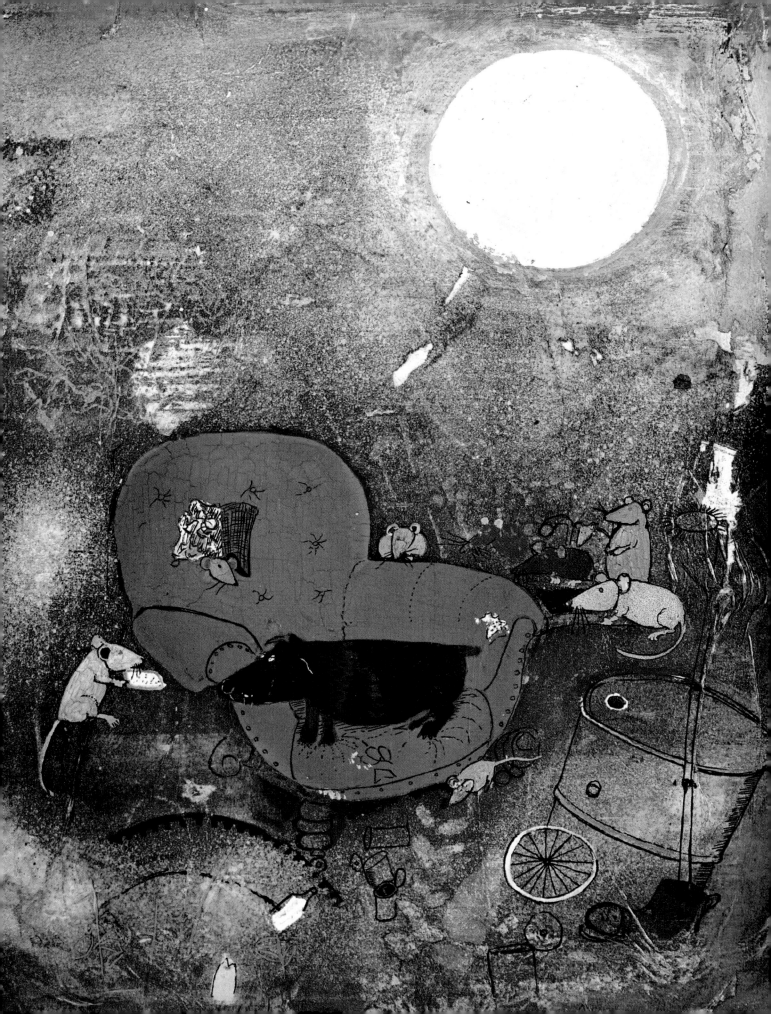

When it was light the next morning, Simp left the
rubbish pit and wandered off in the direction of the
town.  She tried to make friends with people who were
going to work, but nobody seemed to care about her.
She spent a long time searching for something to eat, but
she could not find anything.

Then she came across
some dustbins. She
started looking through
them for food and did
not notice the cats
who were angrily
watching her.

"That's my dustbin," hissed one of the cats as he pounced. Simp ran for her life with the cat just behind her. She was running so fast that she did not look where she was going.

"Got you," said the dog-catcher. Two large hands grabbed Simp, and she was put in the back of the van with the other strays that the dog-catcher had collected. Almost all the other dogs in the van had homes. "We often get picked up," they said. "But what will become of you with no home to go to? And you don't even have a collar."

Simp became more and more worried as she talked to the other dogs. "Who can tell what may happen to you now?" one said. "You're not very pretty, are you?" said another. "I doubt if anybody will want to give you a home," said a third.

The van pulled into the yard of the dog pound. The doors were opened and the dogs driven toward the kennels. When the dog-catcher was looking the other way, Simp saw her chance. She jumped up on some boxes and was away over the wall.

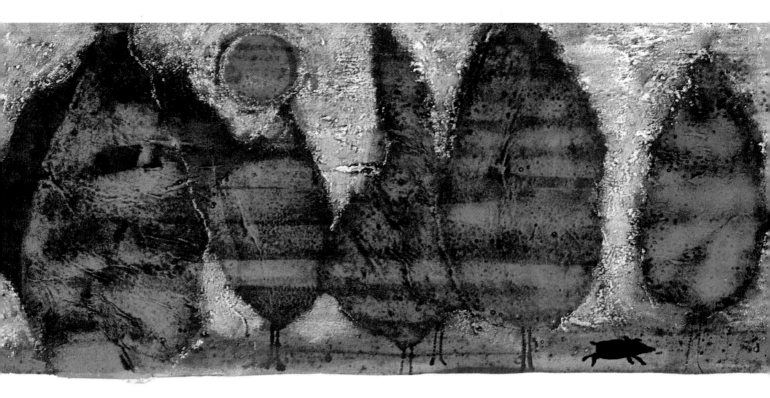

Simp kept running and running until she was well out of town. Then, because she was still frightened, she crept into some thick bushes to hide. By the time it was dark she had become very hungry and set off again down the road.

Then, in the distance, Simp saw lights. They were the lights of a circus.

She went toward them, hoping she might find someone
there who would give her some food.

Perhaps after that she could curl up under a caravan
where it would be a little warmer.

She crept up to a trailer, climbed on a box, and looked through the window. Inside was a clown who was very surprised to see a little dog peering at him. He opened the door and beckoned to Simp.

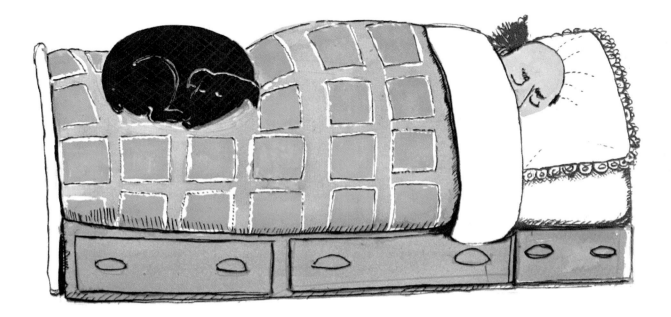

"You look very tired and hungry," said the clown, and he gave Simp a large meal, which she gobbled up. It was warm and comfortable in the caravan, and the clown let Simp lie on his bed. She was soon fast asleep.

The next morning the clown showed Simp around the
circus. There were many tents, caravans and animals.
Simp met a young elephant and a lion.

Everybody seemed happy and friendly, but the clown was worried. People did not like his act anymore.

The clown told Simp exactly what he did. He showed her the cannon that fired a rubber ball through a paper hoop. Just then the ringmaster came up. "Unless you improve your act by tonight, you'll have to go," he said to the clown.

Simp had an idea. "That rubber ball is exactly the same size as me when I am curled up," she thought. "I just have time to work out a plan before the show starts."

The evening performance had begun.  Just before the
clown's act, Simp climbed into the cannon while nobody
was looking.  The man who was to fire the cannon
peered inside and, seeing Simp curled up, thought she was
the ball.  Simp's heart was beating fast as she waited for
the exciting moment to arrive.

The circus managers had a look of boredom on their faces as they watched the clown. "He'll really have to go," they said.

There was a rolling of drums and ...

# WHOOOOOOOOOOOOOSH!

Through the air flew Simp, straight for the paper hoop.
Right through the hoop she went.

The crowds roared with delight when they saw that the "cannonball" was a little black dog. The clown was so surprised to see Simp that he almost dropped the hoop.

Simp landed on a drum and stood there proudly while the audience cheered and cheered. She had really enjoyed being fired from the cannon. Then the clown and Simp were put on a horse and they went round and round the ring. Everybody was still wildly clapping and cheering.

After the show, the ringmaster gave a party for Simp and the clown. He invited the little elephant, the lion, and the monkey Simp had met, and they all ate until they were quite full. The ringmaster told the clown and Simp that their act was the best the circus had ever had.

And so Simp lived happily with the clown and travelled around the countryside with the circus. The act became famous, and people came especially to see the little dog fired from a cannon.

And that is how she came to be called Cannonball Simp.